ZOE
AND THE
MYSTERIOUS X

by Richard Thompson

illustrated by Ruth Ohi

Annick Press, Toronto, Canada

Annick Press gratefully acknowledges
the support of The Canada Council and
the Ontario Arts Council.

Canadian Cataloguing in Publication Data

Thompson, Richard, 1951–
    Zoe and the mysterious x

ISBN 1-55037-081-2 (bound).—ISBN 1-55037-080-4 (pbk.)

I. Ohi, Ruth.   II. Title.

PS8589.H65Z36 1990   jC813'.54   C89-095030-X
PZ7.T46Zo 1990

Distribution for Canada and the USA:

Firefly Books Ltd.
250 Sparks Avenue
Willowdale, Ontario
M2H 2S4

Printed and bound in Canada

For Grandma

There was a big white "X" painted on the road outside Zoe's house.

"I wonder what that "X" means," said Zoe one day.

"It means there's a pirate treasure buried there," Melissa told her.

"Pirates sail in ships," said Zoe. "We aren't even close to the ocean."

"They brought the treasure in an airplane," said Melissa. "They landed at the airport. Then they took a taxi . . ."

"No, you're wrong," said Steven. "That "X" was put there by a giant practicing his ABC's."

"No, that's not right at all," said Becky. "My brother gets X's like that on his school papers all the time. It means a mistake. Something is wrong with that road!"

And it turned out that Becky wasn't the only one who thought there was something wrong with that road.

A week later, a man came to the door of Zoe's house.

"I guess you been wondering about that big white 'X' out on the road," he said.

Zoe nodded.

"Well, it seems someone made a serious mistake with that road," he said. "Here, let me show you."

He unrolled a big sheet of blue paper with white lines on it.

"You see that line? And those numbers there? And this number over here? You know what that all adds up to I guess . . ."

"Four?" suggested Zoe.

"Well, not exactly," said the man. "That road will have to be moved."

"Where are you going to move it to?" asked Zoe.

"It's going to run right through here," said the man.

"You're going to make a road through our house!" yelled Zoe. "You can't do that!"

"Well, not by myself," said the man. "But with a little help from my friends . . ."

And at that very moment, three bulldozers, two graders, six gravel trucks, a backhoe, two packing machines and a paving machine came snorting down the street and stopped right on top of the big white 'X'.

When the machines were done with their work there were four lanes of clean new pavement running right through the middle of Zoe's house.

At first Zoe thought it was kind of neat having a road in her house, but after about two days she changed her mind.

Logging trucks, moving vans, buses, dump trucks, cement trucks, cars, motor homes, and motorcycles roared up and down the road all day and into the night. Zoe couldn't sleep.

Zoe wasn't allowed to cross the road by herself. She had to wait for her mom or dad to take her across to the bathroom.

Truckers rumbled into the kitchen and ordered bacon and eggs,—"the eggs over easy and the bacon crisp."

Tourists stopped and got out of their cars to take pictures.

Families in station wagons parked in their living room to watch TV and wanted to know where they could buy popcorn and licorice.

When there was construction on the road, all the traffic had to detour right through Zoe's bedroom.

A policeman gave Zoe a ticket for speeding on her tricycle.

And a pickup truck got stuck in her sandbox.

Zoe's dad said, "Well, the road's here to stay, so we might as well make the best of it."

They asked Zoe's grandma to come and live with them to be a crossing guard.

They painted a sign and hung it by the kitchen: ZOE'S ROADSIDE DINER.

Then, when truckers rumbled in to order bacon and eggs, they charged them $2.95.

Zoe and her mom and dad took turns. Sometimes Zoe was the cook, sometimes she was the server, and sometimes she washed the dishes.

In the evenings and when she wasn't helping someone get to the bathroom, Zoe's grandma made popcorn and sold it at ZOE'S TWILIGHT DRIVE-IN THEATRE.

They did a booming business and everyone was happy—tired but happy—until . . .

One morning, Zoe and her grandma were waiting to cross the road to the bathroom when a truck roared by. Something flew out of the window and landed—SPLAT!—on Zoe's grandma's head.

"A banana peel, Grandma!" cried Zoe. "That guy threw a banana peel out of his window. That's littering."

"I've been noticing a lot of litter on the road lately," said Zoe's grandma in a sad voice.

Zoe looked around and saw that the road really was getting very messy—bottles and papers and old boots all over the place.

"I don't mind being a crossing guard and selling popcorn," said Zoe's grandma, "but I am not going to be pelted with garbage."

The next day she packed up and went home.

"Grandma's right," said Zoe's mom. "I like working in the diner, but I don't like living in a garbage dump!"

"What are we going to do?" asked Zoe's dad.

They counted the money they had made from selling bacon and eggs and popcorn, but there wasn't enough to buy a new house.

"And nobody will want to buy this messy place," said Zoe's mom. "What ARE we going to do?"

That night, as she lay in her bed listening to the trucks and cars whizz by, Zoe had an idea.

She got out of bed, took a jar of white paint and a fat brush and tiptoed out to the side of the road. When there were no cars or trucks coming either way for as far as she could see, she dashed out into the road and painted a big white 'X'.

Two days later, a man came to the house.

"I guess you been wondering about that big white 'X' out on the road," he said.

Zoe nodded.

"Well, it seems someone made a serious mistake with that road," he said. "Here, let me show you."

He unrolled a big sheet of blue paper with white lines on it.

"You see that line? And those numbers there? And this number over here? You know what that all adds up to, I guess . . ."

"You have to move the road?" suggested Zoe.

"Exactly!" declared the man.

"When are you going to start?" asked Zoe.

"Here come the bulldozers now," said the man.

And at that very moment, three bulldozers, two graders, six gravel trucks, a backhoe, two packing machines and a paving machine came snorting down the road and stopped right on top of the big white 'X'.

When the machines were finished with their work, the road was gone from the middle of Zoe's house.

Once in a while, a logging truck or a bus still gets
lost and comes driving up on Zoe's lawn. When that
happens, Zoe pokes her head out the window and
says, "Go a kilometer down that way, and turn left.
Go straight ahead, and right through the middle of
Becky's house. You can't miss it. 'Bye!''

MARVEL
THE AVENGERS

» THE S.H.I.E.L.D. FILES

Written by
Scott Peterson

Based on Marvel's *The Avengers*
Motion Picture Written by
Joss Whedon

Illustrated by
Lee Garbett, John Lucas,
and
Lee Duhig

Based on
Marvel Comics'
The Avengers

MARVEL
NEW YORK

www.marvel.com

TM & © 2012 Marvel & Subs.

Published by Marvel Press, an imprint of Disney Book Group. No part of this book may be reproduced or transmitted in any form or by any means, electronic or mechanical, including photocopying, recording, or by any information storage and retrieval system, without written permission from the publisher. For information address Marvel Press, 114 Fifth Avenue, New York, New York 10011-5690.

Printed in the United States of America

First Edition

3 5 7 9 10 8 6 4 2

G658-7729-4-12065

ISBN 978-1-4231-5478-5

The things you're about to read are real.

You won't believe it, but it's true.

I'm going to tell you the story of **the Avengers. . . .**

The invincible Iron Man. A red and gold knight in a shining suit of armor.

Tony Stark is the man beneath the iron. He's one of the richest people in the world. Owner of Stark Industries. Inventor of half of the coolest things the world has ever known. Most of all: the creator of the Iron Man suit.

Bullets bounce off it. It can fire repulsor blasts that would knock down a small building.

Oh, and it can fly.

Things weren't always perfect for Tony.
While driving through enemy territory, his truck was blown up and a piece of metal hit Tony's heart.

He was captured, and while a prisoner **he built the first Iron Man armor.** His chest plate acted like a new heart, keeping him alive. And the armor made him strong enough to escape and beat the bad guys.

Back home, Tony decided to fight for those who couldn't fight for themselves. He also fought against super-powered villains bent on total destruction. With a heart of iron and armor to match, Tony Stark was the perfect fit for S.H.I.E.L.D.'s new team.

Next up is the creature known as the incredible Hulk. Eight and a half feet tall and a thousand pounds of attitude.

And he's green.

He can punch through a brick wall. He can rip a tree out of the ground. He can throw a truck like it's a baseball, and he can stomp a tank in half. Plus, he can jump more than a mile.

He doesn't say much, but he yells a lot. It's hard to believe the **Hulk is actually Bruce Banner**, **a brilliant scientist.**

When General Ross, the father of Bruce's girlfriend, said they wanted to cure something called gamma radiation poisoning, Bruce said they could experiment on him.

But General Ross was really trying to create another Super-Soldier like Captain America. It didn't work. Instead of getting Cap's powers, Bruce turned into the Hulk.

Now whenever he gets mad, Bruce changes into the incredible Hulk.

Then there's Thor. Like the Hulk, he is impossibly strong—if there's a limit to his strength, we haven't found it yet.

He carries something he calls Mjolnir—a magical hammer. This hammer cannot be broken—but it seems it can break anything, except for Captain America's shield. No one else can even lift Mjolnir, but if Thor twirls it really fast and then throws it while holding on to its strap, he can fly.

You could say he's . . . mighty.

Thor doesn't wear a special suit, and he wasn't given some Super-Soldier Serum.

Thor is from Asgard, a place of Norse myth that happens to be real.

And while that sounds silly, it's what Thor believes. Also, S.H.I.E.L.D. hasn't found any proof yet that it's not true. So as long as he's one of the good guys, I don't really care where he came from.

His evil brother, **Loki,** on the other hand, is a master of magic and very dangerous—he's number one on our Most Wanted list.

And then there's Captain America.

The ultimate Super-Soldier.

The fastest people can run a mile in three and a half minutes—Captain America can do it in just one. The strongest people can lift a thousand pounds—Captain America can lift twice that. He can't be poisoned or gassed and he almost never gets tired.

And he carries a shield made of vibranium, which cannot be broken.

Yet Captain America was once the smallest, slowest, weakest kid in school.

Young Steve Rogers was smart and nice and tried hard—harder than anyone else. But he was always sickly.

More than anything, Steve wanted to be a soldier. After being rejected again and again, a scientist asked if he would be part of a secret experiment called **Project: Rebirth.** That experiment turned him into the Super-Soldier he is today.

And now Steve Rogers is Captain America, the First Avenger. Cap fights a never-ending battle against evil, which includes the sinister HYDRA organization and its leader, the Red Skull!

Natasha Romanoff. Tony Stark knew her as Natalie Rushman when she worked for him. But, actually, she was working for me. **I call her Black Widow.**

She's an expert in every form of fighting and an expert with every kind of weapon. She speaks a dozen languages. She's even a world-class dancer.

The thing Black Widow may be best at? Keeping everyone guessing—even me. No one can ever tell what she's going to do next . . . but whatever it is, she'll succeed.

And that brings us to Clint Barton—Hawkeye.

Whenever I can't afford to miss, I call in Hawkeye. He is an expert marksman—especially when it comes to archery.

I've seen him do stuff with a bow and arrow that just doesn't seem possible. I mean, Thor was amazed by some of the things Hawkeye could do—and it's not easy to impress a Norse god.

And then there's me. I'm the guy who knows what's going on. The guy who makes things happen.

I run the Strategic Homeland Intervention, Enforcement, and Logistics Division. We just call it S.H.I.E.L.D.

The few people who know me call me **Nick Fury.**

But I think of myself as the man who assembled **the Avengers.**